Henry Holt and Company
Publishers since 1866
120 Broadway, New York, NY 10271
mackids.com

First picture book edition—2013 / Designed by Véronique Lefèvre Sweet
The artist used acrylic and gouache on Fabriano paper to create the
illustrations for this book.
Printed in China by Toppan Leefung Printing Ltd., Dongguan City,
Guangdong Province

10 9 8 7 6 5 4 3

Library of Congress Cataloging-in-Publication Data
Brown, Barbara.
Hanukkah in Alaska / Barbara Brown ; illustrated by Stacey Schuett. —
First picture book edition.
        pages   cm
"A version of this text was first published in 1998 by Henry Holt and Company
in the anthology A Hanukkah Treasury, edited by Eric A. Kimmel."
Summary: A little girl describes the short, harsh days of winter in Alaska
and her efforts to keep a moose from destroying trees and the swing
in her back yard, which she finally succeeds in doing with the help of a
Hanukkah treat. Includes facts about Hanukkah and the aurora borealis.
ISBN 978-0-8050-9749-8
[1. Winter—Fiction. 2. Moose—Fiction. 3. Hanukkah—Fiction.
4. Auroras—Fiction. 5. Jews—United States—Fiction. 6. Alaska—Fiction.]
I. Schuett, Stacey, illustrator. II. Title.
PZ7.B81276Han 2013   [E]—dc23   2013003166

Code 1122/B1309/AA6

For Tim and Sophie
  —B. B.

For O. R.
  —S. S.

In Alaska, in winter, we have to watch out for moose. We have to look both ways when we go out the door, making sure there are no moose around. That's because moose are very big, and they kick things that surprise them or make them angry. Their big kicks are strong enough to dent a car.

My mother drives slowly in the winter,
looking out for moose.

When my friends and I are playing outside
and a moose comes along, we have to hug a
tree. A moose can't step on you or knock you
over if you're hugging a tree.

Also, during winter in Alaska, it's dark.
Not just at night for sleeping, but almost all
the time. It doesn't get light until it's already
snack time at school, and it's dark again
practically right after lunch. Daytime is only
five hours long. And sometimes, when there's
so much snow that it covers up the windows,
daylight can barely peek in.

Alaska snow piles up everywhere. It gets
so deep that the moose with their skinny legs
have trouble walking in it. They like to use
people's cleared driveways and paths.

That's why a moose lives in our backyard. He wandered up our driveway, found a good spot where he could nibble at our trees, and decided to stay. He sleeps in our yard and eats our trees. I try throwing carrots to him, even cookies, but he really likes the tree with my blue swing on it.

I'm worried about my swing. Once, we saw a moose walking around town with a swing in his antlers. He'd gotten tangled and just tore the whole swing away.

I think the dark and that moose are making me kind of grumpy, because even Hanukkah hasn't cheered me up. My friends and I pretend to be dreidels spinning in the snow, and when the mail lady comes, she always has another present for me from my aunts and uncles Outside. (Do you know that everywhere else from Alaska is called "Outside"?)

But every time I light a new candle in our menorah, I look out the window and it's still dark, and that moose is still there, too close to my swing and eating our trees. My mother and I throw some apples, hoping he'll like them instead, but he just watches them fall and eats more tree.

One night as I am lighting the last Hanukkah candle, my father says, "Let's go outside. I have something to show you."

"With the moose there?"

"Don't worry. We'll stay far away."

I put on my long underwear and two layers of socks.

I put on my thick, baggy sweatpants . . .

and a sweatshirt.

I put a snowsuit on
over all that, two layers
of mittens, and a hat.

Still, it's freezing cold outside, and it's very dark,
and I do not like being anywhere near that moose.
I want that moose away from my swing!

"Just wait. You'll see." But he's looking at the sky.

I'm looking at that moose.

My mother says, "Maybe we can try some fresh spinach. Maybe he'll leave your swing alone for something green."

But the spinach doesn't work, and I'm freezing.

Dad says, "This is a perfect night. You'll see."

Suddenly, Dad points up to the sky. There are pink and purple and orange ribbons of light, swirling and shining and glowing. Against the dark black of the sky, the lights are bright and beautiful. I have never seen anything like this. So much light, and so big. Filling the sky. A rainbow on black velvet.

"They're called the northern lights," Dad says. "Aurora borealis. They happen especially up here in Alaska, but only when the sky is just right. Our very own Hanukkah Festival of Lights."

It looks like ribbons of wax, all the candles from all the menorahs, melting into the dark, lighting it up. I stare at those lights. I stare so hard, I don't even notice the moose sticking his head through my swing.

Next thing I know, the moose is yanking on the chain, pulling on the whole tree. CREAK! CLANK! SNORT! I can't stand it. That moose will tear everything up.

But then I have an idea. I run into the
house and run back outside with my hands full.
I wave what I have at the moose, and he sniffs, turning
his head away from the swing. I back up, laying what I have
down in the snow. The moose stretches his head, reaches for it.
I keep backing up, laying more down, and the moose follows
me! Out of the yard, down the driveway, AWAY! I lay the last
batch down and race back into our yard.

I look at the sky, at the lights. I'm so happy to
see those lights. I'm so happy that moose is gone.
My parents are surprised. "What did you feed
him?" they ask. "What did he like so much?"

"Latkes," I answer.

Hanukkah can be
pretty funny in Alaska,
and miracles can happen
in a lot of different ways.

The Story of Hanukkah*

The story of Hanukkah happened a long, long time ago in the land of Israel. At that time, the Holy Temple in Jerusalem was the most special place for the Jewish people.

The Temple contained many beautiful objects, including a tall, golden menorah. Unlike menorahs of today, this one had seven (rather than nine) branches and was lit not by candles or light bulbs, but by oil. Every evening, oil would be poured into the cups that sat on top of the menorah. The Temple would glow with shimmering light.

At the time of the Hanukkah story, a cruel king named Antiochus ruled over the land of Israel. "I don't like the Jewish people," declared Antiochus. "They are so different from me. I don't celebrate Shabbat or read from the Torah, so why should they?" Antiochus ordered the Jewish people to stop being Jewish and to pray to Greek gods. "No more going to the Temple, no more celebrating Shabbat, and no more Torah!" shouted Antiochus. He sent his guards to ransack the Temple. They brought mud and garbage into the Temple. They broke furniture, tore curtains, and smashed the jars of oil that were used to light the menorah.

This made the Jews very angry. One Jew named Judah Maccabee cried out, "We must stop Antiochus! We must think of ways to make him leave the land of Israel." At first, Judah's followers, called the Maccabees, were afraid. "Judah," they said, "Antiochus has so many soldiers and they carry such big weapons. He even uses elephants to fight his battles. How can we Jews, who don't have weapons, fight against him?" Judah replied, "If we think very hard and plan very carefully, we will be able to

defeat him." It took a long time, but at last the Maccabees chased Antiochus and his men out of Israel.

As soon as Antiochus and his soldiers were gone, the Jewish people hurried to Jerusalem to clean their Temple. What a mess! The beautiful menorah was gone, and the floor was covered with trash, broken furniture, and jagged pieces from the shattered jars of oil. The Maccabees built a new menorah. At first they worried that they would not be able to light their new menorah, but they searched and searched, until at last they found one tiny jar of oil—enough to light the menorah for just one evening. The Maccabees knew that it would be at least eight days until they could prepare more oil, but they lit the menorah anyway. To their surprise, this little jar of oil burned for eight days. The Jewish people could not believe their good fortune. First, their small army had chased away Antiochus' large army, and now the tiny jar of oil had lasted for eight whole days!

The Jewish people prayed and thanked God for these miracles. Every year during Hanukkah, Jews light menorahs for eight days to remember the miracles that happened long ago.

---

* The transliterated word *Hanukkah* can be spelled in a number of different ways—including *Chanukah, Chanuka,* etc.